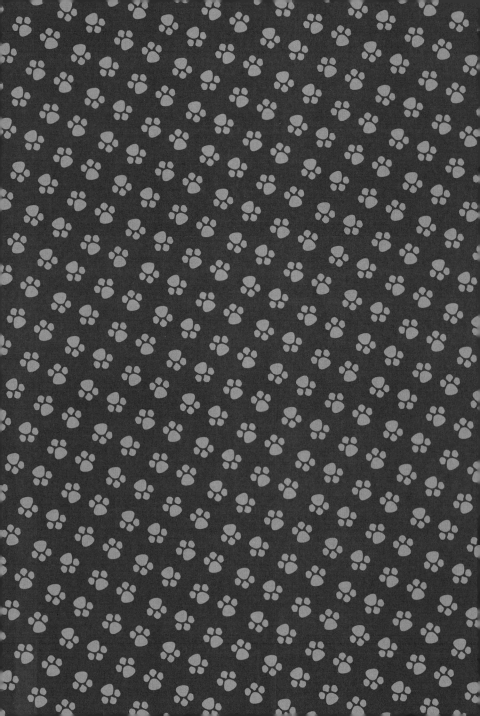

HELPER HOUNDS

Robot

Helps Max and Lily Deal with Bullies

Dedication
To my husband, Rafi.
Thanks for sharing and encouraging my love of the bully breeds!
And again, to the fine people at Hinsdale Humane Society.
Thanks for taking care of so many of the inspiration-dogs for these stories.

HELPER HOUNDS

Robot

Helps Max and Lily Deal with Bullies

Caryn Rivadeneira

Illustrated by Priscilla Alpaugh

RED CHAIR
·PRESS·

Egremont, Massachusetts

RED CHAIR PRESS
BOOKS FOR YOUNG READERS

www.redchairpress.com

Publisher's Cataloging-In-Publication Data

Names: Rivadeneira, Caryn Dahlstrand, author | Alpaugh, Priscilla, illustrator.

Title: Robot helps Max and Lily deal with bullies / Caryn Rivadeneira ; illustrated by Priscilla Alpaugh.

Description: Egremont, Massachusetts : Red Chair Press, [2020] | Series: Helper hounds | Summary: "Max and Lily are being teased and bullied at school. Their Aunt Eileen calls the Helper Hounds – and soon Robot, an endearing Rottweiler who knows all about bullies, comes to give support"-- Provided by publisher.

Identifiers: ISBN 9781634407762 (library hardcover) | ISBN 9781634407793 (paperback) | ISBN 9781634407809 (ebook)

Subjects: LCSH: Rottweiler dog--Juvenile fiction. | Human-animal relationships--Juvenile fiction. | Bullying--Juvenile fiction. | Brothers and sisters--Juvenile fiction. | CYAC: Rottweiler dog--Fiction. | Human-animal relationships--Fiction. | Bullying--Fiction. | Brothers and sisters--Fiction.

Classification: LCC PZ7.1.R57627 Ro 2020 | DDC [E]--dc23

Library of Congress Control Number: 2019951547

Photos: iStock

Printed in the United States of America

0520 1P CGF20

CHAPTER 1

A flash of brown rumbled past the window.
I stretched my paw and rolled my best tennis
ball toward my mouth. I chomped the ball into
position and jumped onto the window seat.

I knew it! The brown truck was right in front
of Ms. Chen's house. The lady in brown shorts
ran toward Ms. Chen's house.

Ms. Chen! Ms. Chen! I chomped and barked
my best warning. But it was no use. Ms. Chen
opened the door, smiled, and took a tan box
from the woman in brown.

Noooooo!

"Robot!" Samuel said. "What's going on?"

Samuel put his hand on my back and leaned into the window with me. Ms. Chen waved at the woman in brown shorts.

"Aah, worried about Ms. Chen, Robot?" Samuel said. "Good thing she has you to help scare away those trucks."

Samuel scratched my ears and told me to sit. I sat. He wiggled my best ball out of my mouth and tossed it across the living room.

"Get it," Samuel said.

I sprung off the window seat and got the ball. I plopped it at his feet and sat.

Samuel turned the ball in his hands. He squeezed it. A crack opened into a wide smile.

"Sure you don't want to play with a *new* ball?" Samuel said.

I was sure. I stuck my tongue out and wagged my stubby tail.

Samuel shook his head. He and I had been over this before. Sometimes Samuel would

throw me one of the
bright yellow tennis
balls from my
basket. I would go
get it. But I never
choose those balls.
It takes a long
time—a lot of chomping
and barking and
slobber—to get a tennis
ball *this* good.

Samuel threw the ball. I ran to get it. So I
dropped the ball at Samuel's feet and sat—just
waiting for the next throw. I could do this all
day. But before he could throw it, Samuel's
phone buzzed. *A Helper Hounds Alert!*

Samuel grabbed his phone. He frowned and
plopped onto our old green sofa.

"Oh no," Samuel said.

I munched up my ball and crawled onto the

sofa next to him. He scratched my head.

"Two kids—Max and Lily—are being bullied!" Samuel said. "I hate when kids are mean to each other."

Samuel used to be a teacher. He'd seen a lot of kids getting bullied.

Samuel scrolled down on his phone.

"One kid tells Max he's skinny and that he could snap him in two. Another girl makes fun of Lily because Max and Lily don't live with their mom right now. Terrible!"

I barked my agreement.

Samuel held my snout in his hands and kissed my nose. He walked to the hallway where my official red Helper Hounds vest and leash hung on hooks. My stubby tail wagged.

"Can you help these two learn to stop their bullies?" Samuel said.

My tail wagged so hard my butt shook the sofa cushion. I jumped off.

I could help! I knew all about dealing with bullies. Two reasons:

1. I'm a Rottweiler. That means, I'm big and loud. Some people think I'm a bully! But it also means that I was born and bred to *protect*. My great-great-great-great-great grandparents protected sheep from bully bears and mountain lions in Germany. Today, I protect Ms. Chen and Samuel from the bully brown trucks! I'm always on alert for bullies.

2. My foster dad and trainer, Paul, was a bully. Well, he *was* a bully. Now, Paul is the nicest guy ever! But once upon a time, Paul did some really bad bully things— and ended up in prison. That's where I met him. For real! I'll tell you all about how we both got there. Let me go back to the beginning.

CHAPTER 2

I don't remember much before the morning of "the raid." My brothers, sisters, and I climbed over one another to get closer to our mom, Mama Petunia.

Not that we were ever far away. All seven of us dogs lived in a tiny wire cage at "Flowerbrook Kennels." It might sound nice, but it wasn't. The people at Flowerbrook Kennels kept dogs in cages. We ate, peed, pooped, and slept all in the same place.

At least the puppies got to leave. The mom dogs never did. They spent their whole lives in cages, having puppies and then caring for us. The mom dogs never played or put their paws in the grass. No one ever pet them—or loved them. Well, except for us puppies.

And then, people from the pet stores would come with big vans and big boxes and move the puppies to their stores. The pet stores sold the puppies for lots of money. At least, that's what Samuel tells me. So, it's true.

Most of the families who bought the puppies from the pet stores never knew how bad it was at Flowerbrook Kennels. The pet stores said puppies came from "good" breeders.

That was a lie.

When Samuel and I visit schools and libraries and hospitals, Samuel tells people about the lies pet stores tell.

"Adopt, don't shop!" he says. I hope people listen.

Anyway, my brothers and sisters and I were some of the very last puppies born at Flowerbrook Kennels. Turns out, one of the pet store workers felt bad about getting puppies from such a terrible place and called the police.

The police called the humane society. And one day, police and animal rescue volunteers came rumbling onto the farm with cars and

trucks and vans. The people at Flowerbrook Kennels didn't use cars so we knew something was up. We all had our snouts through the wires in the cages to sniff the air.

A woman with a sweet smile and soft voice came up to our cage and put my siblings and me in a big blanket. She gently set us in a clean, warm crate in the back of a van. Another man put my mom in a blanket and held her on his lap up front. The man called my mom "Sweet Little Mama Petunia." Mama Petunia stopped crying when he said that.

We all stopped crying and barking when we got to our new foster family's house. A foster family, our van driver told us, steps in to take care of you when your parents can't.

"And you need to let your Mama Petunia get some rest," she said.

Our foster mom came out to the van to get us. She hugged and kissed Mom all over and told her she'd make her "better." I didn't know how Mom could get any better (she was pretty great already). But the rescue people seemed worried about her. Mom had trouble standing up.

At our new house, Mom got to spend lots of time on a cushy round bed in the kitchen. Julia, the nice woman at our foster home, gave her bits of chicken and bowls of fresh water. Living her whole life at the terrible kennel made Mom sick. So, Julia tucked Mom under big blankets—with her very own teddy bear!

We got teddy bears too. And we got stuffed llamas and squeaky pigs and tug ropes. But the best thing we got were tennis balls. I fell in love right away. The smell. The color. The *squish* as I tried to sink my paws and puppy teeth into it! I loved it all.

Julia noticed how much I loved to chase the ball. As I grew, she would teach me to "sit" and go "down"—and used the ball as my reward. I would do anything for that ball!

I loved living with our foster family. But we didn't stay there too long. They needed to get Mom feeling better—and to help us find new homes. The good news was that lots of people wanted to adopt Rottweiler puppies.

The even better news was that Julia thought I would make a good "service dog." I didn't know what that was, but if it meant more tennis balls, I was in!

So one day, Julia brought me to Mom, who lifted her head and sniffed me all over. She gave me one big lick to say goodbye. She was a good mom. I was going to miss her. But dogs like me are meant to go off into the world—and do big things!

So I went to prison. Where I would learn to be a good dog. A service dog!

CHAPTER 3

Paul and I met in the big fenced-in yard. I liked Paul right away. He smelled like sweat and ink. His arms and neck were decorated in blue stripes and squiggles. His bald head shined in the sun.

But I wasn't sure he liked me! At least, not when he first squatted down to meet me.

"Paul," Julia said. "Meet Robot."

"You're a little fuzzy guy now," Paul said. "But soon you'll be a big dude like me!"

I sure hoped so!

"I hear you like to play with tennis balls," Paul said. He reached into his sweatshirt and got a… tennis ball! My stubby tail shook my whole body.

"You think you can learn to be a service dog?" Paul said.

He held the ball above my head. I looked up to see it. My bottom went down.

"Good boy!" Paul said.

"Good boy!" Julia said.

Paul and Julia pet me and talked for a while. Then, Julia kissed me on the snout and said good-bye. It wasn't very sad. I liked this guy Paul.

Paul scooped me up into his stripy arms and kissed me on the head. I liked all these kisses. They made me feel like everything was going to be okay. Paul waved one arm around and held me in the other.

"Welcome to your new home," Paul said. "Let's see what we can make of you. This place sure made something out of me!"

Paul took me for a walk around the "yard"

and then into our room. It was perfect. The room was small, with white walls and one tiny window that let in light and breeze. All along the walls and the door that clicked shut behind us were pictures of puppies, of Paul, and of dogs with badges.

In the corner next to Paul's bed was a crate. Paul knelt down and led me toward it. He tapped the inside with his hand. Paul gave me a tiny treat for just watching this!

I walked in slowly, sniffing everything. I found a soft cushion, a bowl of water, a stuffed pig, a tug rope, and a tennis ball! Heaven.

Paul and I got to work right away. And then we worked every day!

My first lesson was to learn the basics— how to sit, go down, rollover, stay, come, heel. Each time I did something right, Paul clicked a clicker and then slipped me a tiny treat.

But at the end of a great lesson—after I did

a bunch of good stuff in a row—Paul would
throw me the tennis ball. I'd chase it around
toward the door of our room and tumble all
over it. Paul would pick it up for me, hold it up
in his hands, and then tell me to sit. When I sat,
he would throw it again.

Paul also taught me how to ring a little bell
when I needed to "go potty." I had to learn to
use the yard for my bathroom. That was okay.
I didn't like peeing in the rain. But Paul stood
next to me so it was okay.

As the days went by, I got bigger and bigger. And I learned more and more tricks. I got really good. Pretty soon I was able to do all my commands without Paul saying anything. He would just move his hand, and I would sit or stay or heel or sit pretty. Whatever he asked me to!

By then, a click of the clicker told me I did a good job. A toss of the tennis ball told me our lesson was over and it was time to play!

Play time was my favorite. Paul said he wished we could be back in his house—the place where he grew up. The place where his mom still lived.

"I could throw this ball clear through the woods and into the stream," Paul said. "You and I would have fun splashing in that stream."

I was sure we would! But playing in this yard was pretty great too.

Paul liked to tell stories about his mom's house and about when he was a boy. He told lots of them at night when the guard yelled, "LIGHTS OUT!" and boom! Our room went dark.

Paul would stretch on his bed. I would curl up on mine. And Paul would talk and talk and talk.

Most of the stories were good. I heard all about the stream and the woods and Paul's brother Bill and his cousins. I heard lots about Paul's dogs Skipper and Rowdy.

Some of the stories were sad. They made Paul cry. I hated being stuck in my crate when Paul cried. I wanted to scoot up close to him and stick my snout under his arm to make him laugh. I wanted to lick his face to let him know it was going to be okay.

But prison has lots of rules. And the rules said I had to stay in my crate at night. So I just listened. One night Paul told me the story of how he got to prison.

This was one of Paul's sad stories.

CHAPTER 4

Paul was a good kid. Back when he played with Bill and skipped rocks with his dog Skipper. Paul liked to play at the creek because it was quiet. Back home, Paul's dad yelled a lot. Paul's dad threw glasses and punched walls. It was scary at home.

Then one day, Paul's dad left home. At first, Paul was happy about it. The house was as quiet as the creek. Well, except for his mom's tears. But then Paul felt sad. Then, he felt mad.

That's when Paul started picking on the kids in his class.

He called kids "fat" and "stupid" and "ugly." He pushed kids in the hallway. He stole lunches.

He made fun of everyone.

Paul was bigger than the other kids so everyone was scared of him. Nobody stopped him! Being mean made Paul feel powerful. So, he kept being mean.

One day, a new teacher arrived. The first time Mr. Tuttle saw Paul push another student, Mr. Tuttle told him to stay after.

Mr. Tuttle grounded him from recess for a week. Then he told Paul he had a choice. Paul needed to decide what kind of person he wanted to be: a bully or a friend. Mr. Tuttle offered to help him learn how to be a friend.

But Paul just laughed at him. Paul wanted to be a bully.

As Paul got older, he kept doing mean things. Until one day, when Paul was nineteen, Paul robbed an old man's house. The man came home early and surprised Paul on the stairs. Paul pushed the man and ran out of the house. The man fell down the stairs, hit his head, and almost died.

Paul went to prison. That was twenty years ago.

Don't worry! The story gets happier.

Not long after Paul got to prison, Paul got a letter. It was from his old teacher: Mr. Tuttle! Paul couldn't believe it. Mr. Tuttle said Paul could still make a choice. Paul needed to decide what kind of person he wanted to be: a bully or a friend. If Paul wanted to be a friend, Mr. Tuttle could help.

This time, Paul didn't laugh. He cried and cried in his cell. Paul had no friends. Paul didn't want to be a bully anymore. He was lonely. Paul needed help.

Paul wrote Mr. Tuttle. *They* became friends. And Mr. Tuttle helped Paul learn how to be a friend to others. Paul learned how to say nice things to people. Mr. Tuttle helped Paul learn the power of forgiveness and how to apologize. Then, Paul wrote letters to the kids and the adults he had been mean to.

"I was a bully," Paul wrote in note after note. "I am sorry. Please forgive me."

Some people wrote back and said they forgave him. Some never wrote back. But that was okay. Paul was learning how to be a friend to others and to be a good person in the world.

Soon, Mr. Tuttle talked to the prison warden (the boss!). He asked if Paul could join the prison's new dog-training program.

As it turns out, Mr. Tuttle had retired from teaching and started training rescue dogs. His first dogs became the first Helper Hounds. Mr. Tuttle was a Helper Human!

Long story short: Paul learned how to train dogs. Before me, Paul helped Labradors and pit bulls, poodles and mutts. They became police dogs, search-and-rescue dogs, sniffer dogs, and service dogs.

And some dogs even got to become Helper Hounds. Sometimes we became Helper Hounds because we were "too friendly" to be police dogs. Sometimes we became Helper Hounds because our sniffers were not that great. Other times, we became Helper Hounds because we had "something extra." That's what Mr. Tuttle called it.

Mr. Tuttle had an "eye" for this. He saw that "something extra" in Paul way back in seventh grade. Mr. Tuttle showed Paul how to spot the something extra in people and in dogs. And Paul saw it in me.

That's when Paul called Mr. Tuttle. "I think Robot is your next Helper Hound," Paul said.

Mr. Tuttle came the next week. He put me through some tests. He made lots of loud noises and ran past me. He told me to sit and to stay and then threw my tennis ball. I didn't move.

Mr. Tuttle smiled.

Then he sat on the ground and pretended to cry. I knew Mr. Tuttle was faking. But I nuzzled up close and licked his face. Then I sat super still while Mr. Tuttle hugged and leaned into me.

I forgot to tell you: In the year I spent with Paul, I got big. Really big! I weigh over 100 pounds now. That means I am good for humans to lean on.

Mr. Tuttle hugged me and kissed my snout.

Then, Mr. Tuttle took my picture, tapped on his phone, and threw up his hands in a "release." My test was over. I trotted back to Paul. He was crying for real. Paul knelt down and told me how good I was. Paul leaned his forehead against mine.

"You get to be a world-famous Helper Hound, Robot," Paul said. He wiped his eyes. "I'm going to miss you. But I am so proud of you. Now..."

Paul slipped my "Pup-In-Training" vest off. Mr. Tuttle gave him a red Helper Hounds vest. Paul put it on me and smiled.

I found out later that the other Helper Hounds had to graduate from Helper Hounds University before they got their vest. But I got "private lessons," Paul joked.

"You go help people," Paul said. "Be a good

friend. Make this world a better place. Do it for me."

Paul knelt back down for a hug. I licked his face so he knew it was going to be okay. I leaned into him and wagged my stump. He tipped back and laughed.

"And remember: you're a big guy!" Paul laughed. "Don't bump the little kids over!"

Mr. Tuttle said they would work on that when we went to Helper Hounds University for real.

Then he shook Paul's hand and said, "You are a good friend and a good man, Paul. You did good work with Robot. I'm proud of you."

"Thanks, Mr. Tuttle—er, Samuel," Paul said. "For so much." Paul sniffled again.

"You're welcome," Mr. Tuttle said.

I stood next to Paul and waited to head back into our room.

But then Mr. Tuttle picked up a bag with my stuffed pig, my blanket, and my tennis balls. Mr.

Tuttle clipped my leash on my new vest and off we went. I turned to look back at Paul. He stood in the yard and waved. A light breeze blew by. I could smell his inky arms and salty tears.

I wanted him to come with us! But Paul had to stay in prison. That was sad. Paul was a good friend.

But the story doesn't stay sad. Trust me! We will get back to that. But first, we need to get back to our story. Max and Lily are waiting.

CHAPTER 5

Samuel pulled the Helper Hounds van along a curb and looked up at a long row of houses. They all looked alike.

"Let's see," Samuel said, inching the van forward. "675, 677, 679…ah, here we are. 681. This is the place. This is where Max and Lily live."

Samuel straightened my vest and opened his door. I snatched my tennis ball out of the cup holder and followed Samuel out of the van. I chomped my ball and stuck my nose in the air. *Sniff. Sniff. Sniff.* I always like to get a sniff of a place. Helps me relax. That, and squishing my ball of course.

As I sniffed a tree on our way up to the door, the door opened. A girl and boy stood between the frame. Max and Lily! Max smiled at me. Lily stared at me and scowled.

A man tapped the kids' shoulders. "Can we make some space here?"

A woman laughed behind him. "Yes, can we make room to welcome our guests?" she said.

Lily flattened herself against the doorway. Max stepped on to the stoop. He didn't lose his smile. Lily didn't lose her scowl.

The man and woman walked right up to Samuel and held out their hands.

"I'm Rico," the man said. "We emailed."

"Great to meet you," Samuel said and shook their hands.

"I'm Max's and Lily's Aunt Eileen," the woman said. "And I told Rico about you."

The adults all laughed. I wiggled my tail and gave my tennis ball two chomps of joy.

"Well, I'm glad you did. It's great to meet you both," Samuel said. "This slobbery guy with the tennis ball is Robot."

I knew the drill, so I sat without being told. Rico put a hand toward my snout. Then Eileen followed. I sniffed them both and tapped each hand with my ball. It always seemed like a polite thing to do.

"What a beautiful dog!" Rico said. "Kids, come meet Robot."

Max stepped forward. Lily didn't move an inch.

"This is Max," Rico said. "Lily? Coming?"

Lily shook her head no. She held her arms tightly crossed against her body.

Max gave me his hand to sniff. His hand smelled like peanut butter and sweat. A kid who likes to eat and play! My favorite kind of kid! I stood up so I could press my head into his stomach. Max seemed like he needed to rub

my head. I found that lots of people did. Max
giggled and put his hand on my head.

"He's soft," Max said. "His head is *huge!*"

"He is and it is," Samuel said. "Just gave him
a bath so I hope he smells okay too."

Max giggled again and bent to sniff my head. "He smells like lemons. A lemon-head!"

Everyone laughed—except for Lily. She stood with arms crossed and her scowl firmly in place. Scowling, arms-crossed kids are also my favorite kind. I like them all! I chomped my ball and tugged my leash.

"Can we go meet your sister?" Samuel asked Max.

"She doesn't like strangers," Max said. "She's pretty shy."

"And angry…" Rico added under his breath. Eileen bumped him with her elbow.

"That's okay," Samuel said. "We can give her space. Where's the best place to talk?"

"Inside," Eileen said. Rico motioned toward the front door.

I'd hoped to sneak a sniff of Lily once I got inside. But by the time we were inside, Lily sat perched on the highest step in the hallway.

CHAPTER 6

Eileen led us into a room full of bookcases, small tables, soft sofas, and cushy chairs. I wasn't allowed on any of them (Helper Hound rules), but I didn't care. This room also had the softest rug I'd ever set paws on.

I wanted to dig my paws into that rug and shove my snout deep into the sofa. But I didn't (Helper Hounds rules again…). Instead, I sat nicely and dropped my ball onto the rug and let my tongue hang so Samuel would notice how much I liked the soft rug.

Max sat criss-cross-applesauce next to me. He giggled and patted my head and back. Lily had come back but watched us from her perch on the top stair in the hallway. Samuel, Rico, and Eileen filled out some paperwork and talked.

"Can I throw his ball for him?" Max asked.

"If it's okay with Eileen and Rico," Samuel said. "Perhaps just *roll* it more than *throw* it."

"*Rolling* the ball is fine with me," Eileen said.

Samuel unclipped my vest so I'd know it was okay to play fetch. Then Samuel told Max how to put me in a sit and then tell me to "get it." Max rolled the ball into the hallway and told me to "get it" like he'd been doing it all his life.

I chased after the ball and let it bounce a couple times against the wall before heading back. I hoped Lily would follow. She didn't. But she did scoot down three steps.

I brought the ball back to Max. He "rolled" it again. Although this time the ball bounced off the floor and onto the stairs.

I chased the ball, grabbed it off the bottom

step, and chomped it a couple times in front of Lily, who had scooted down another step.

"Why does he chomp it like that?" Lily asked. "Is he pretending it's someone's head?"

"Goodness no!" Samuel said as he twisted on the sofa so he could see Lily. "It's like his pacifier, really. You know how babies get calmer when they have a pacifier in their mouths? Same with Robot. That disgusting old tennis ball helps him relax."

Lily nodded. "Why does he need to relax?" Lily asked.

"Actually, he doesn't," Samuel said. "Helper Hounds *are* relaxed, so you might say chomping his ball is more of a habit. But the ball helped him a lot during his stressful puppyhood."

"Why was it stressful?" Max asked.

"Well, first of all, Robot was born in a puppy mill," Samuel said.

"What's that?" Lily asked.

"It's a place where people force dogs to have litter after litter of puppies. The mom dogs are kept in cages. Most never even get to feel the grass."

"Who would get a puppy from a place like that?" Eileen asked.

"Anyone who's ever bought a puppy from a pet store gets their dog from a place like this!" Samuel said.

"That's awful!" said Rico.

"How'd he get out?" Lily asked. "Did you buy him at a pet store?"

"Heavens, no," Samuel said. "Robot, his brothers and sisters, his mom, and about 100 other puppies and dogs were rescued from a puppy mill and sent to live with foster families."

"Like us," Max said.

Lily nodded and moved down another step.

"Does Robot get to see his mom?" Lily asked.

"He does!" Samuel said. "His mom was

really sick from living in the puppy mill. She had a hard life—and almost died. But her foster family saved her. Robot's mom, Mama Petunia, lives with them now. We still visit."

"That's like us too," Max said. "We'll see our mom next week. She's getting better."

"Better every day, sweetie!" Eileen said. "You should be very proud of your mom. She's working hard because she loves you so much."

Max smiled and nodded. He tossed the ball for me again. Lily got to the ball first. She sat on the bottom step by now and reached out her hand with the ball. I took it from her with my best "soft mouth." No teeth! Just like Paul had taught me. Lily smiled and scratched my shoulder.

"But I bet no kids ever tease you and call you names because you don't live with your mom," Lily said.

I could smell Lily's tears before I saw them.

So, I gave her two slurps
on her cheeks to let
her know it would
be okay.

Max joined us in
the hallway.

Max said: "And I bet
a big dude like you never gets teased
or tripped because you're 'so skinny you might
just *snap in two.*'"

It was true. I didn't get teased for not living
with my mom—and no one ever told me I
was too skinny. (The vet says the opposite.
Something about needing to watch how many
snacks I get….) But I slurped Max on the knee
to let him know it would be okay too.

I wished I could tell Max and Lily two
things:

1. Just like dogs, people come in all shapes
   and sizes. And that's good! Being big

helps me do my guard-dog thing. But the skinny dogs? They can run faster and get comfortable in smaller places.

2. My foster parents—first Julia and then Paul—were the best people ever. They loved me and taught me when my mom couldn't. And Samuel—my forever dad— would never have found me if it weren't for Paul. I'd never be a Helper Hound without Paul!

But before I could figure out how to tell them this, I heard a familiar rumble. I chomped up my ball and trotted toward the front door. They'd left it open. Just a thin screen between me and what I knew was coming: The Brown Truck!

I woofed two of my best barks before Samuel told me to sit and hush. But the brown truck stopped right in front of Max and Lily's house. *Danger! Danger!*

CHAPTER 7

I grabbed my ball and whipped my head back to Lily and Max. If they would stay put, I could save them from the brown-suited driver.

But when I turned back, Lily stood right next to me, her hand on my back. I chomped my ball and ruffed my best barks.

Thank goodness, the driver ran toward the house next door and back to her truck as fast as she could. Saved again. By me and my bark. Samuel walked into the hallway to reward my good-boy-ness with a liver treat. Next to my tennis ball, this was my favorite.

"Why'd he bark at the delivery lady?" Lily asked.

"Any guesses?" Samuel said.

"He wants to bite her?"

"Not exactly," Samuel said. "Robot doesn't want to bite anyone. But Robot *does* want to protect us. Rottweilers are guard dogs. It's in their nature to 'speak up' when they sense danger. And that's the right thing to do. When Robot barks, I know something might be wrong. In this case, it's just the delivery truck. But sometimes, it's real danger. Robot helps by talking—or, barking and chomping."

Lily laughed.

"It's true," Eileen said and patted the sofa cushion next to her. "Talking does help. So, how about you all come back in here and we'll talk."

Lily put her hand on my back and walked into the living room with Max and me. I plopped down on the fluffy rug. Lily and Max sat criss-cross-applesauce next to me.

"You did the right thing by telling Eileen and

Rico about the bullies," Samuel said. "I was a teacher for a long time. I dealt with a lot of kids who said and did mean things. I know some good ways to stop them. Wanna hear?"

Max and Lily nodded.

"OK," Samuel said. "Three things, super simple:

1. Tell the kids to stop what they're doing.
2. If they don't stop, tell the kids they are being bullies by not stopping when you asked.
3. If they *still* don't stop, tell a grown up. This part feels scary! But it's important that you tell your teacher, principal, mom, foster-parents, relatives, or any trusted adult.

Bullies *expect* us to keep quiet. That's why telling Rico and your Aunt Eileen was so smart and brave."

"What about telling a Helper Hound?" Lily said. "Can that be one of the steps?"

"Yeah, is it good that we told Robot?" Max said.

Samuel smiled. "Robot *is* a great listener. You can tell him anything. And Robot sure helps me feel brave."

"Because he's a guard dog!" Lily said.

"Is that why he was in a prison?" Max asked. "To guard prisoners?"

"Not exactly," Samuel said. Samuel told Max and Lily all about Paul. How he used to be a bully but learned how to be a friend and how he started training dogs—like me!

"In fact," Samuel said. "Paul was the one who taught Robot all his best tricks, like this…"

Samuel put up a hand. I sat. Then he waved it down. I lay down. He twirled his pointer finger. I rolled over. Then he brought his hands to his face and smiled. I "sat pretty."

Max and Lily laughed. People always do. I wobble a little when I sit pretty.

"So Paul was able to change?" Lily asked. "He went from a bully to a nice guy?"

"He did," Samuel said. "Not everyone chooses to be nice, but it's worth a try, right?"

Max sighed. "So maybe someday Mike will stop trying to 'snap' me and want to be my friend?"

"Yeah right," said Lily, "I told my teacher. I told our social worker. I told Rico and Eileen. And I told my mom last weekend when she visited. And Jessica *still* calls me Lily NoMama—at school and online. Robot, can you come to school with me to bark at Jessica and make her run away like the delivery lady?"

I chomped my ball twice. If this Jessica were running toward our door with a big box, I sure would! But Samuel had another answer.

"Well," Samuel said, "Robot probably won't bark at Jessica to make her go away. But Robot *can* come to school. And remember, Robot and

I are here because you spoke up. It's already helping!"

"Wait, Robot really could come to our school?" Lily said.

"Could I walk him down the hallway?" Max asked.

"Yes and yes!" Samuel said.

"Rico and I talked to Principal Wayne after we emailed Samuel and Robot," Eileen said. "Robot's coming to do an Anti-Bullying Assembly next week."

Lily and Max smiled at each other. Max reached a hand out to scratch me. But then, Lily's scowl returned.

"Hold on," Lily said. "Then everyone will know we told! Jessica and Mike will get even meaner!"

"I know it's scary," Rico said. "But this is going to help. It's going to help you and Max and all the kids who are getting bullied."

"And it's going to help Jessica and Mike too," Samuel said. "They'll learn a lot from Paul."

"The *prisoner!*" Lily said. "Is he out of jail?"

"Nope," Samuel said. "But Paul uses his time in prison to make the world a better place. So, he trains service dogs and makes videos for the Helper Hounds Anti-Bullying Assemblies. You'll really like Paul. And he and Robot will help. You'll see."

Lily leaned close in to me and whispered: "I just miss my mom…." I slurped her face. I missed my mom too—and Paul. But it *was* going to get better. I couldn't wait to show her.

CHAPTER 8

"May I help you?" a voice said. I looked at the brick wall. Very weird! Then again, I couldn't place the clank-clank sound coming from behind me either. It sounded like the sailboats in the marina we sometimes visited. But I didn't see any sailboats. Now, I heard a voice but didn't see any people!

I turned and turned as I tried to figure out where the voice came from. Samuel told me to sit.

"Yes," Samuel said to the wall. "This is Samuel Tuttle and Robot Tuttle with...."

"Helper Hounds!" the voice said as the door buzzed.

Samuel called me up from my sit, patted my Helper Hounds vest, and pulled the door open. Before walking in, I took one last look around for the source of the clank and the voice in the wall. I turned back to see a circle of people standing in the hallway ahead.

"Mr. Tuttle, such a pleasure," a man said. "I'm Principal Wayne."

A woman knelt in front of me. The voice!

"This must be Robot," the Voice said. "I'm Vicky Callah. I'm the sixth-grade counselor. We've read all about you! I can't believe you're really here."

My stump wagged. While Ms. Callah scratched my neck, the other grown-ups shook hands with Samuel. Some reached down to pet me. Others stood back and just stared. That happens a lot. Not everyone believes a big black dog like me is a helper.

"More like a bully than a Helper Hound,"

one man said under his coffee-breath.

"You should know bullies come in all shapes and sizes, Coach Renway," Ms. Callah said. "And bullying isn't about how someone 'looks' but about how someone behaves. I'm sure you'll learn more about that in the assembly."

"Yes, yes," Principal Wayne said. "Everyone calm down. We all have a lot to learn about bullying today. We're so happy you're here. The bell will be ringing soon. We better get down to the auditorium so you can set up."

Principal Wayne led us down a long hallway and motioned toward the gym, the library, and the doors to the playground. He told Samuel about the history of the school, about the students, and about how *nice* most of the kids were.

Then, the bell rang.

I looked up at the top of the wall. Finally, I could spot the source of a sound!

A tiny hammer hit a red bell faster than a hummingbird's wings. I stared at the bell and tried to thump my stumpy tail fast enough to keep up. But then, I heard a familiar sound and smelled a familiar smell.

Someone was running. Fast. That someone was Max.

I stood up and turned around. Samuel turned with me.

Max bolted down the hallway with a boy not far behind.

"I'm gonna snap you like a twig, Skinny," the boy yelled. "You blabbed and now we have this stupid assembly."

Samuel tapped his fingers and said, "Speak."

I barked. Max looked right at me and skidded to a halt. A smile spread across his face, like a light went off. Max turned around and pointed a finger at the boy. Samuel and I walked up beside him.

"You're right," Max said. "I did tell. I may be skinny. But you're a bully—and you need to stop."

Principal Wayne walked up to Mike and said: "Indeed you do. In fact, you can sit next to me during the assembly. That way, I'll make sure you don't miss anything."

Mike groaned and stared down at me. "A Rottenweiler?" Mike asked.

"That old joke," Samuel said. "You can pet him if you like. There's not a rotten bone in his body."

Mike scratched the top of my head. Most dogs don't like hands on the tops of their heads, but I do. Especially when I can sneak in a quick lick. Mike might act mean, but he needed to know it was going to be okay too.

"Okay," Principal Wayne said. "Mike and I need to have a talk in my office. Can you show Mr. Tuttle and Robot to the auditorium?"

Max smiled and nodded. Samuel handed Max my leash. Max led us to the auditorium. All along the way kids said, "Cool dog, Max" and stopped to pet me. Some asked Max how he knew a world-famous Helper Hound. Max beamed and told kids they'd have to wait till the assembly.

CHAPTER 9

Samuel straightened my vest and handed me my ball. I chomped it twice and then turned around to show it to Max and Lily.

"Wish I had a ball to chomp on," Lily said.

"Me too," Max said. "Might help me relax."

They both shifted in their seats right behind me on the stage. Samuel asked them if they were nervous as we watched the kids file in and fill row after row in the auditorium. They said, "No," but Lily's leg bounced behind me. I leaned against her. Lily put her arm on me and the shaking stopped.

The kids giggled and chatted in their seats until Principal Wayne tapped the microphone.

The room grew still.

"Students of Hilltop Middle School," Principal Wayne said. "We have very special guests here today."

Vicky the counselor stepped up to the podium and said, "Max and Lily Noah became friends with our guests so they will introduce them."

Samuel handed my leash to Lily and told me to stand up. Max took a deep breath. Lily took a step forward.

In front of us, children clapped. Some whistled. I chomped my ball in appreciation. Then the three of us walked to the podium. I sat, gave my ball two chomps, and looked at Lily. Her notes shook in her hands. I scooted closer.

"I'd like to introduce my new friends," Lily said… But before she could continue a girl yelled out: "Lily NoMama doesn't have friends!"

Two girls snickered.

A scowl crossed Lily's red face. Max grabbed Lily's hand. Ms. Callah the counselor stood up and walked toward the podium.

Behind me, Samuel said, "Robot, speak."

I dropped my ball, opened my mouth, and woofed my best woof.

Lily looked at me. The corners of her mouth rose. Her scowl turned into a smile. Lily turned to Ms. Callah. "I got this," Lily said. Ms. Callah smiled and sat back down.

Lily reached down to scratch my head. Then she took my leash from Max and leaned into the microphone.

"I'm *not* Lily NoMama," she said. "And I do have friends *and* a mother. My friend Robot showed me why it's important to speak up against bullying. So that's what I'm going to do."

Lily cleared her throat.

"Jessica, you are a bully," Lily said. "Maybe you don't mean to be one. Maybe you don't know. Maybe you do it because you're sad or angry or lonely. But you need to stop. You can choose right now to be nice or to stay mean. If you choose to stay mean, bad things might happen to you. But if you choose to be nice, you can do good things in the world. Robot and his friends Mr. Tuttle and Paul can help you choose to be nice. So can I, if you want."

The auditorium erupted in cheers. Lily knelt down to hug me. I could smell her tears before I saw them. So I licked her face three times to let her know it was going to be okay.

When the kids settled down, Max officially introduced Samuel and me. Before Max left the podium, he added quickly: "And Mike, stop saying you could snap me. Just be nice for once."

Max was serious, but as he rushed back to his seat, he giggled along with everyone else. Well, everyone except Mike and Jessica.

Mike slumped in his seat during our whole

presentation. While other kids oohed and awwwed at my puppy pictures, Mike frowned. When kids applauded my tricks and practiced "speaking up" against bullying, Jessica stared into space.

At the end of Paul's video, Paul looked right into the camera and gave the kids the same choice Mr. Tuttle offered him all those years ago: "Do you want to be a bully or a friend? Do you want to do good in the world or make it worse? Most of us act mean because we're hurting or scared or angry or because something is wrong in our own world. But we don't have to be mean. Being mean landed me in prison. Not every bully goes to jail. But every bully ends up feeling lost and alone. And that's a kind of prison, too."

When Samuel got up and asked what the kids wanted to choose, everyone yelled, "To be a friend!" Except Jessica and Mike. Then Samuel ended our assembly the way he always did.

"I began Helper Hounds because I wanted to be a Helper Human," Samuel said. "But you don't need to train dogs to do that. Each of you can be a Helper Human. In fact, if you'd like to be one, you're welcome to come up afterward and get your own Helper Human badge. But only if you're serious about choosing kindness and helping others speak up about bullying. If you or a friend is being bullied, you need to speak up: Tell the bully to stop. Then tell a parent, teacher, or trusted adult. It takes a *lot* of courage to do. You have to be braver to stop bullying than to be a bully! Bullies are cowards. But it's the way to make our world better."

After the clapping stopped, Principal Wayne told everyone they were dismissed. Samuel, Max, Lily and I went down by a table where kids lined up. The line was huge. Some kids wanted to talk about bullying. Some wanted to talk about choosing niceness. And everyone wanted a badge! I sat nicely while some kids gave me a quick pat and others walked by with a side-eye glance. Some kids hugged me and practiced speaking up. Others asked to see a trick.

The girl at the end of the line said something else entirely.

"I need to practice something," she told Samuel. "Can I say it to Robot first?"

Samuel smiled and nodded.

The girl wrapped her arms around me and whispered. I smelled tears so I slurped her face to let her know it would be okay.

The girl nodded and approached Lily. "I'm sorry I call you Lily NoMama," she said. "I don't know why I do. My mom isn't around much either…." The girl sobbed and Ms. Callah stepped over.

"How about we talk in my office?" Ms. Callah said.

Then Mike walked up. Max stiffened. Mike looked down at me and then at Samuel.

"So how do I choose to be nice?" Mike asked. "I'm not strong enough to snap you anyway..."

Samuel smiled. So did Max. As the three of them talked, Lily knelt down and hugged me. I didn't smell any tears, but I slurped her face anyway.

"I still miss my mom and I'm still a little mad at Jessica," she said. "But I think it's going to be okay."

I was so glad she understood.

EPILOGUE

Dear Robot:

Mike says hi! Weird thing is: Mike sometimes still calls me skinny. But now when I remind him that he chose to be nice, he apologizes. He's asked me to hang out with him sometimes too. We both love dogs and video games and baseball. I may be skinny but I can hit the ball way further than he can!

My mom says hi too. We saw her last weekend. She's doing great. She should be done with her program in another month. Then, we might be able to spend weekends with her. Hope you can come visit us too. Anyway, I gotta run. Mike just texted in the group chat. He saw a dog that looked just like you down the block. I wanna go see!

Your friend—

Max

Dear Robot:

Jessica and I aren't exactly friends but she did text me to say she was sorry. And, when I passed her lunch table, Jessica smiled at me. Normally that's when she'd call me Lily NoMama. So, that seems like a step. Anyway, another girl named Tish apologized for not speaking up. She's friends with Jessica and said she was bad, too, for not stopping Jessica. So, that was nice. Tish has horses and her mom invited me, Max, Eileen, and Rico over to her farm to visit them. Tish said her horses help kids with trouble walking. She joked that they were Helper Horses! hahahahaha.

Rico and Eileen told me you went to visit Paul. Was it fun to be back at your old "house"? Hope so. I miss my old house. And my mom. Hope I get to see you soon. I have some stuff I want to say to my mom, but I need you to help me practice saying it.

xo—

Lily

Robot's
Rules for Dealing with Bullies

RULE #1:

Tell the bully to stop what he or she is doing.

RULE #2:

If they don't stop, tell the person they are being a bully by not stopping when you asked.

RULE #3:

If they *still* don't stop, tell a grown-up. It's important to tell your teacher, principal, mom, foster parents, relatives, or any trusted adult.

Bullies think they can scare you into being quiet and not telling someone. But telling someone is being brave.

FUN FACTS

About Rottweilers

Robot, the dog in this story, is a big, strong, loving protector. That's what most Rottweilers are like. These dogs can look scary and tough, but they are usually gentle and loyal.

The Rottweiler has been around for a long, long time. Thousands of years ago, Roman soldiers traveled across Europe. They brought big dogs with them to herd their cattle. At one time, the Roman army and their dogs camped near what is now Germany. After the soldiers left, some of the dogs were left behind. They herded sheep and cattle. They even hunted bears! Later, this part of

Germany became the town of Rottweil. The Rottweilers we know today are descended from these ancient dogs and got their name from the town where they lived.

By the early 1900s, there wasn't as much need for herding dogs. That's when Rottweilers got a new job. They became guard dogs and police dogs. Many also served in the army. These dogs are very protective and smart. They really care about protecting people. And because they are so big and strong, they were good at scaring away bad guys!

Rottweilers might look tough, but they are really very sweet. Rotties, as they are often called, love to lean against people they like. This is their way of showing love and protection. Also, despite their big size—a male Rottie can weigh up to 135 pounds (61 kg)—these dogs like to cuddle. Many Rottweilers think they are lap dogs and will happily climb onto their favorite person for a snuggle.

Sadly, many people are scared of Rottweilers. They think these big dogs will hurt them or want to fight. Although some Rotties do fight, that is because their owners trained them to be mean. Most of these dogs are playful and loving. As with any dog, it is important to treat Rottweilers with respect.

Rotties may look big and tough, but, like Robot, most of these dogs just want to be your friend and playmate. A Rottie is just a big bundle of love.

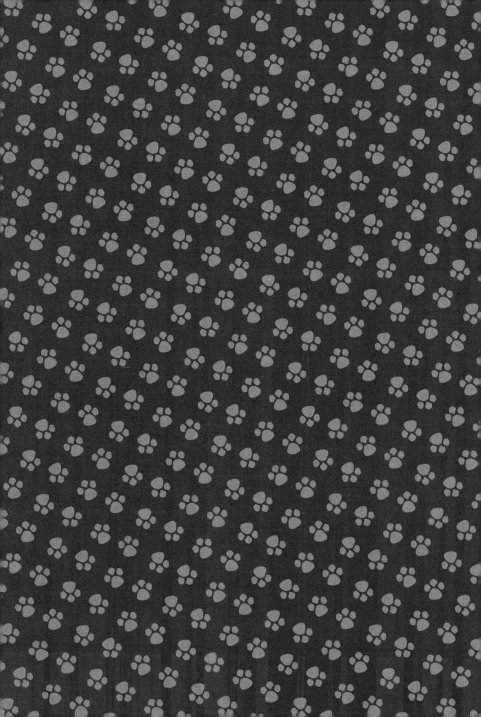